GUINE

PE
PI

And Then There Were Gnomes

COLLEEN AF VENABLE

ILLUSTRATED BY
STEPHANIE YUE

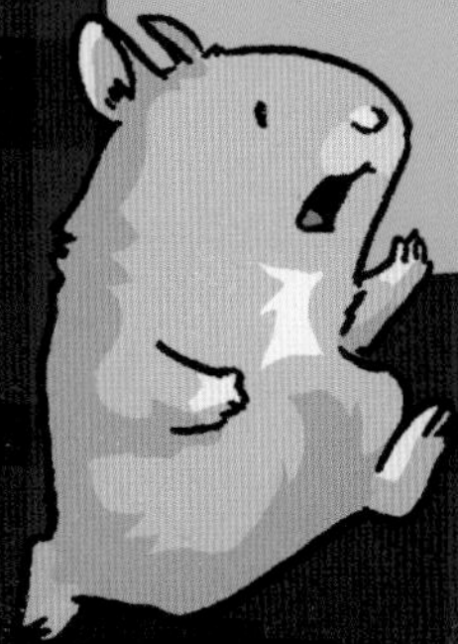

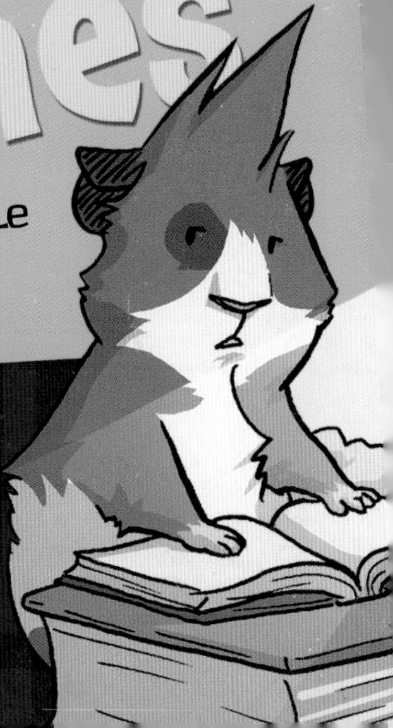

GRAPHIC UNIVERSE™
MINNEAPOLIS • NEW YORK

Story by Colleen AF Venable

Art by Stephanie Yue

Coloring by Hi-Fi Design

Lettering by Zack Giallongo

Graphic Universe™
A division of Lerner Publishing Group, Inc.
241 First Avenue North
Minneapolis, MN 55401 U.S.A.

Website address: www.lernerbooks.com

Library of Congress Cataloging-in-Publication Data

Venable, Colleen AF.
And then there were gnomes / by Colleen AF Venable ; illustrated by Stephanie Yue.
p. cm. — (Guinea PIG, pet shop private eye ; #02)
Summary: Sasspants, the reluctant guinea pig private investigator, is drawn into another mystery by Hamisher the hamster who believes there is a ghost in the pet shop.
ISBN: 978–0–7613–4599–2 (lib. bdg. : alk. paper)
1. Graphic novels. [1. Graphic novels. 2. Mystery and detective stories. 3. Guinea pigs—Fiction. 4. Hamsters—Fiction. 5. Pet shops—Fiction. 6. Animals—Fiction. 7. Humorous stories.] I. Yue, Stephanie, ill. II. Title.
PZ7.7.V46And 2010
741.5'973—dc22 2009020896

Manufactured in the United States of America
1 – DP – 7/15/10

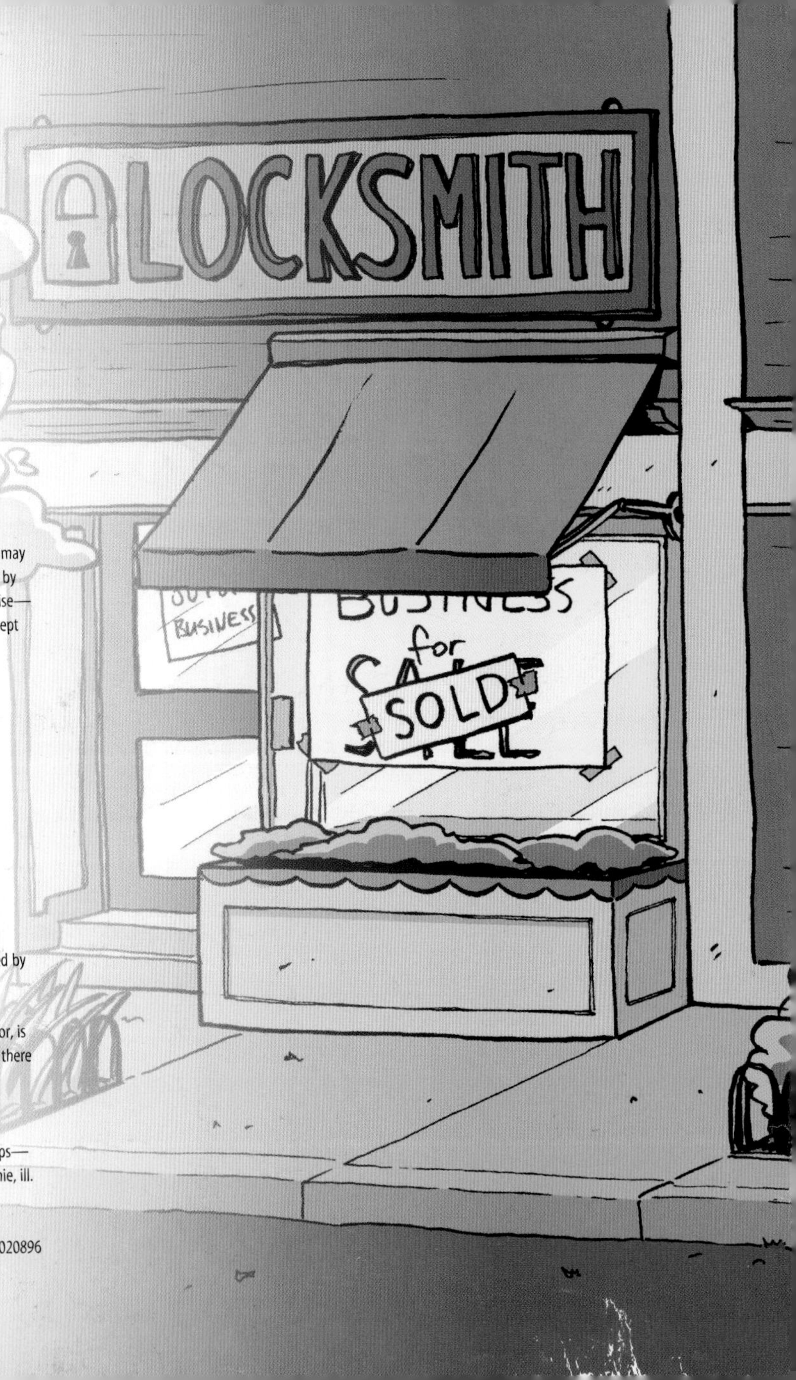
LOCKSMITH
BUSINESS
for
SOLD

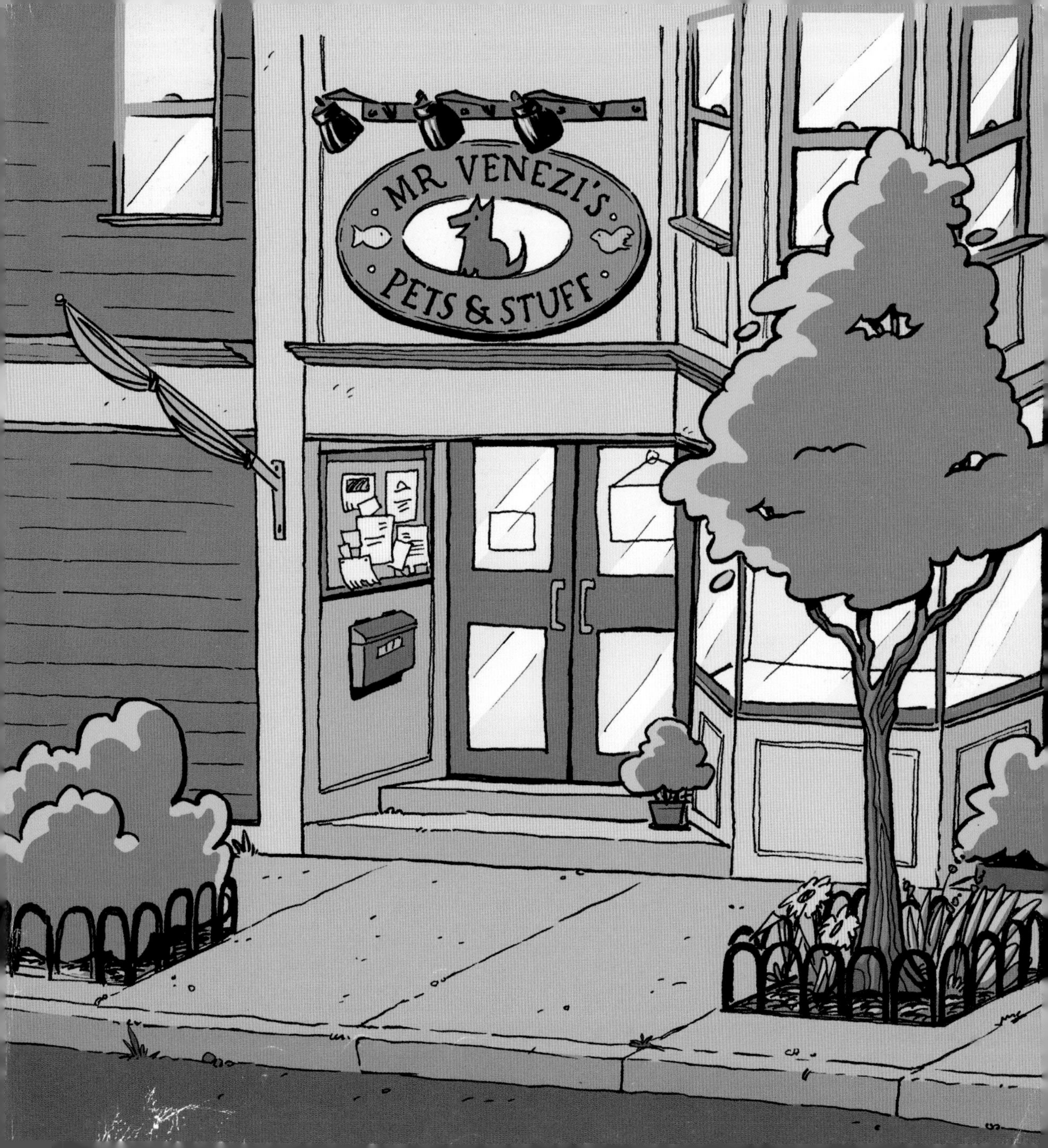
MR. VENEZI'S
PETS & STUFF

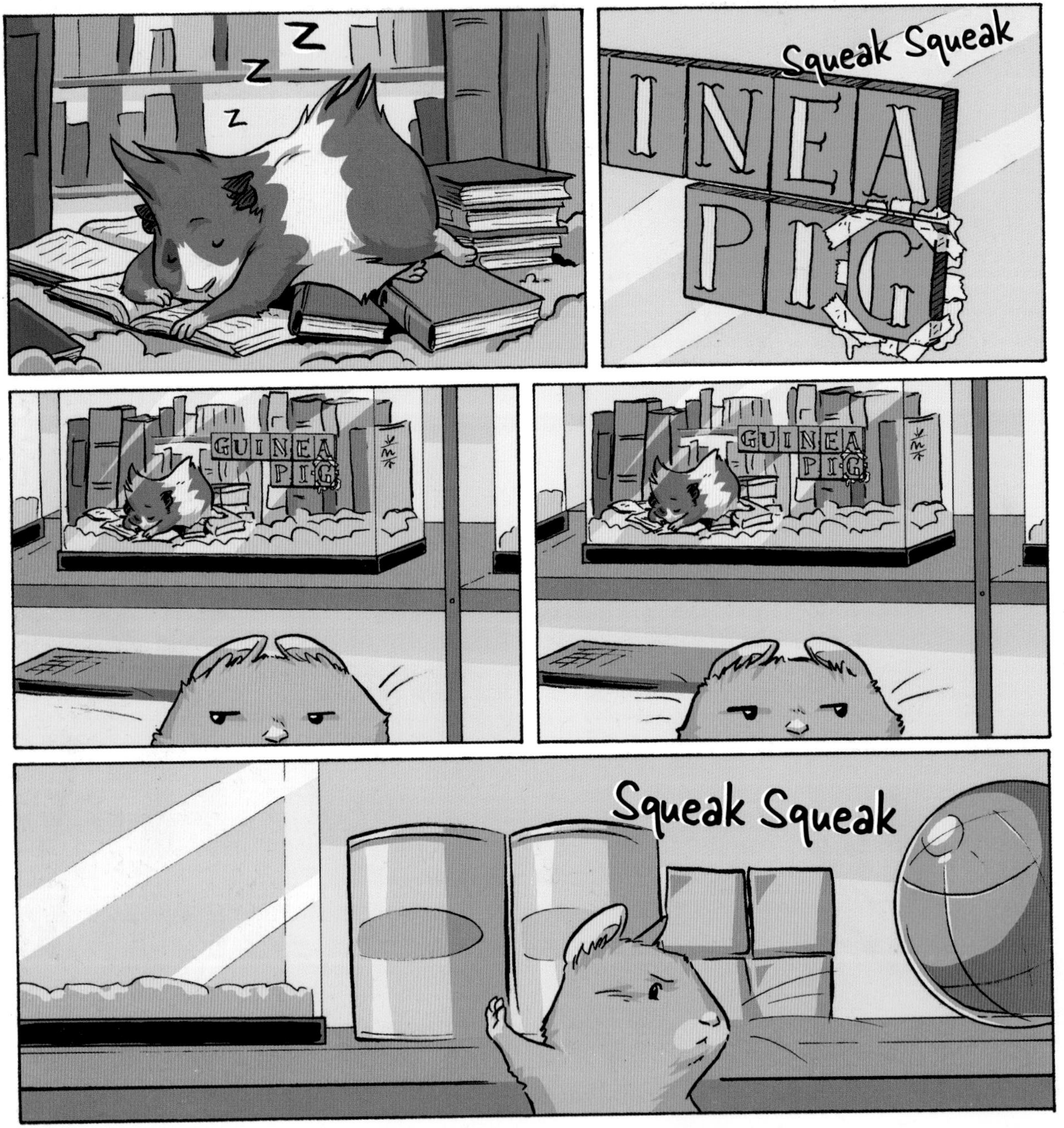
Z
Z
Z
Squeak Squeak
INEA
PIG
GUINEA
PIG
GUINEA
PIG
Squeak Squeak

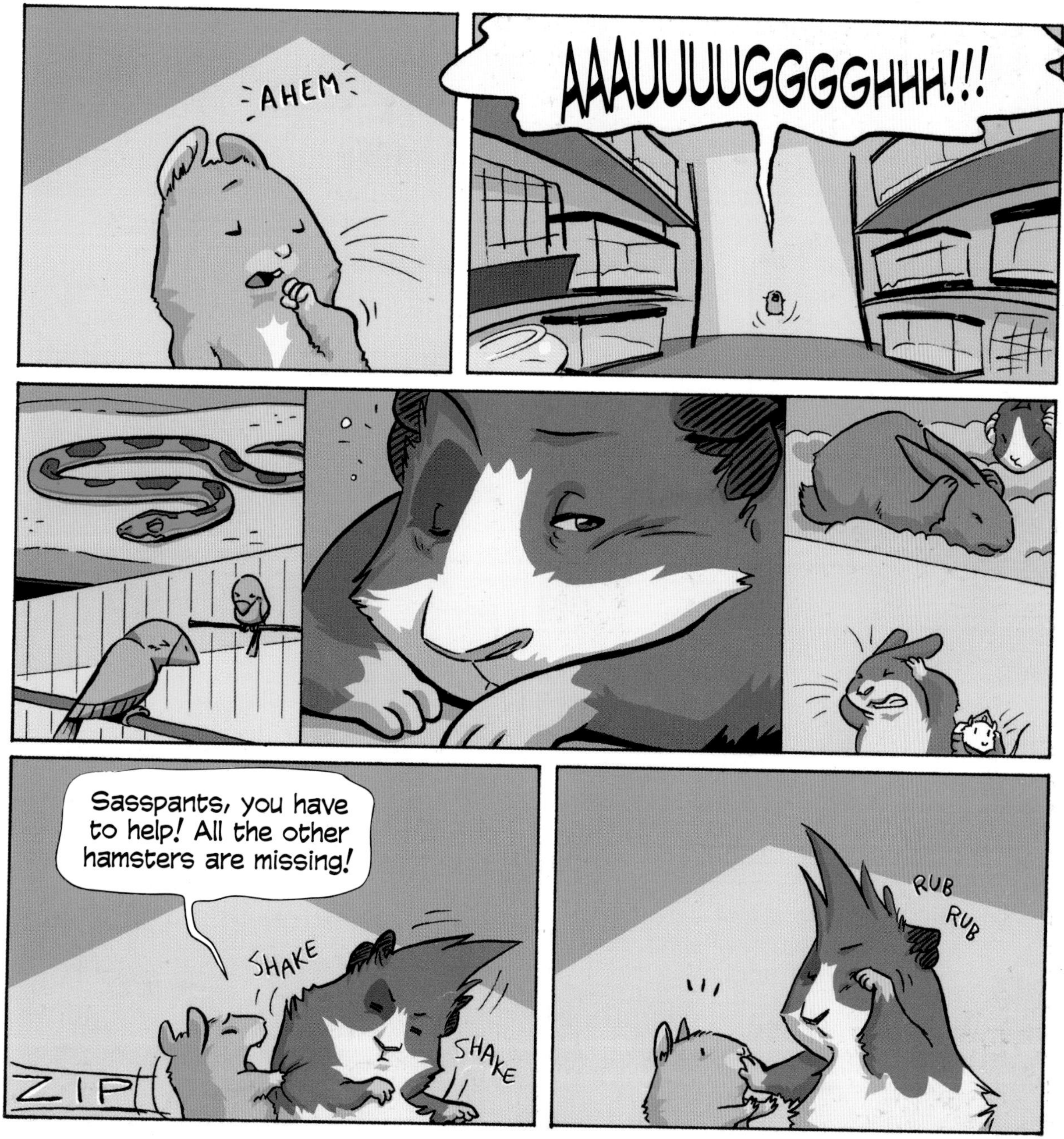
AHEM
AAAUUUUGGGGHHH!!!
Sasspants, you have to help! All the other hamsters are missing!
SHAKE
ZIP
SHAKE
RUB
RUB

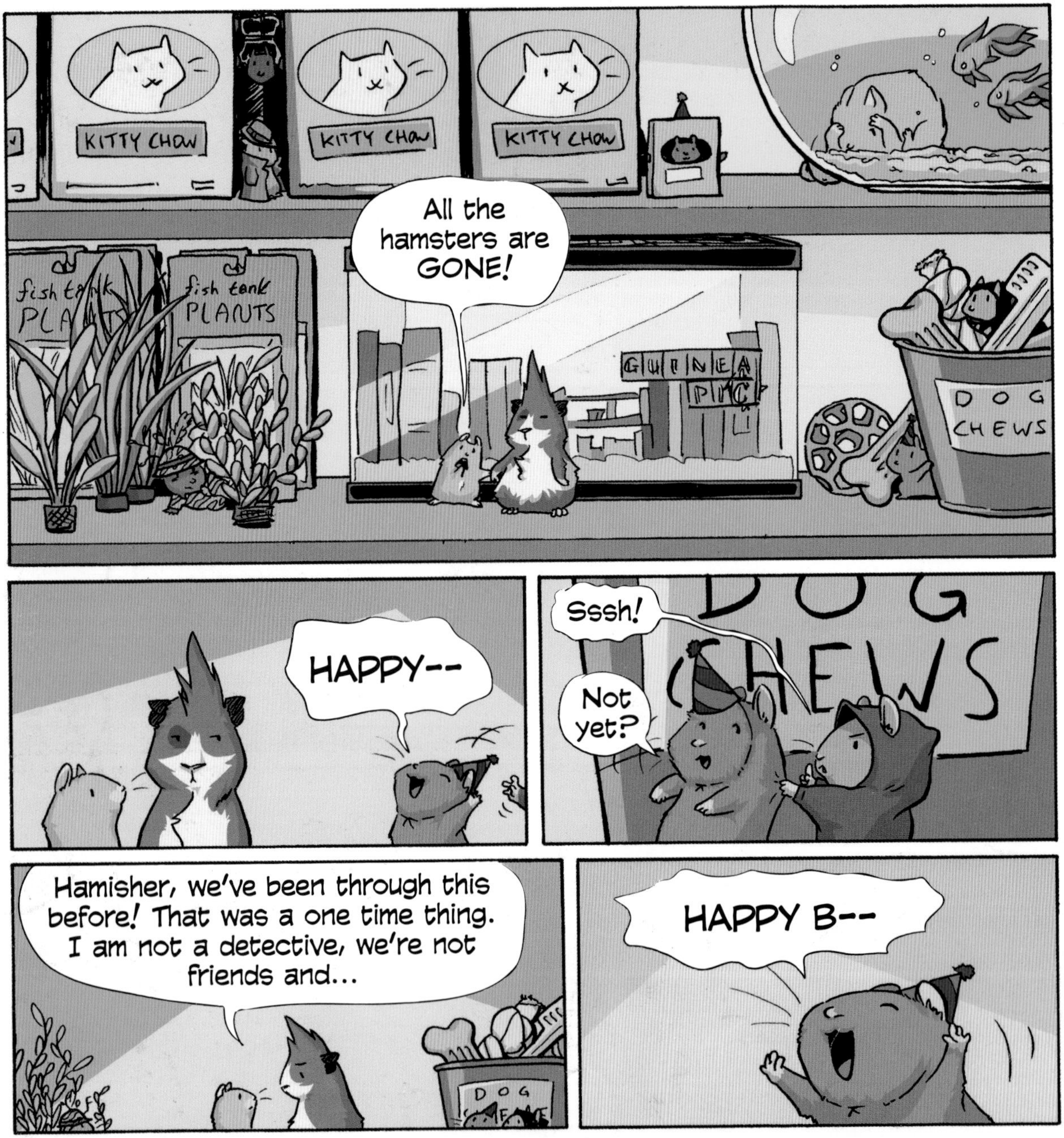
KITTY CHOW
KITTY CHOW
KITTY CHOW
fish tank PLANTS
fish tank PLANTS
All the hamsters are GONE!
GUINEA PIG
DOG CHEWS
HAPPY--
Sssh!
Not yet?
DOG CHEWS
Hamisher, we've been through this before! That was a one time thing. I am not a detective, we're not friends and...
HAPPY B--

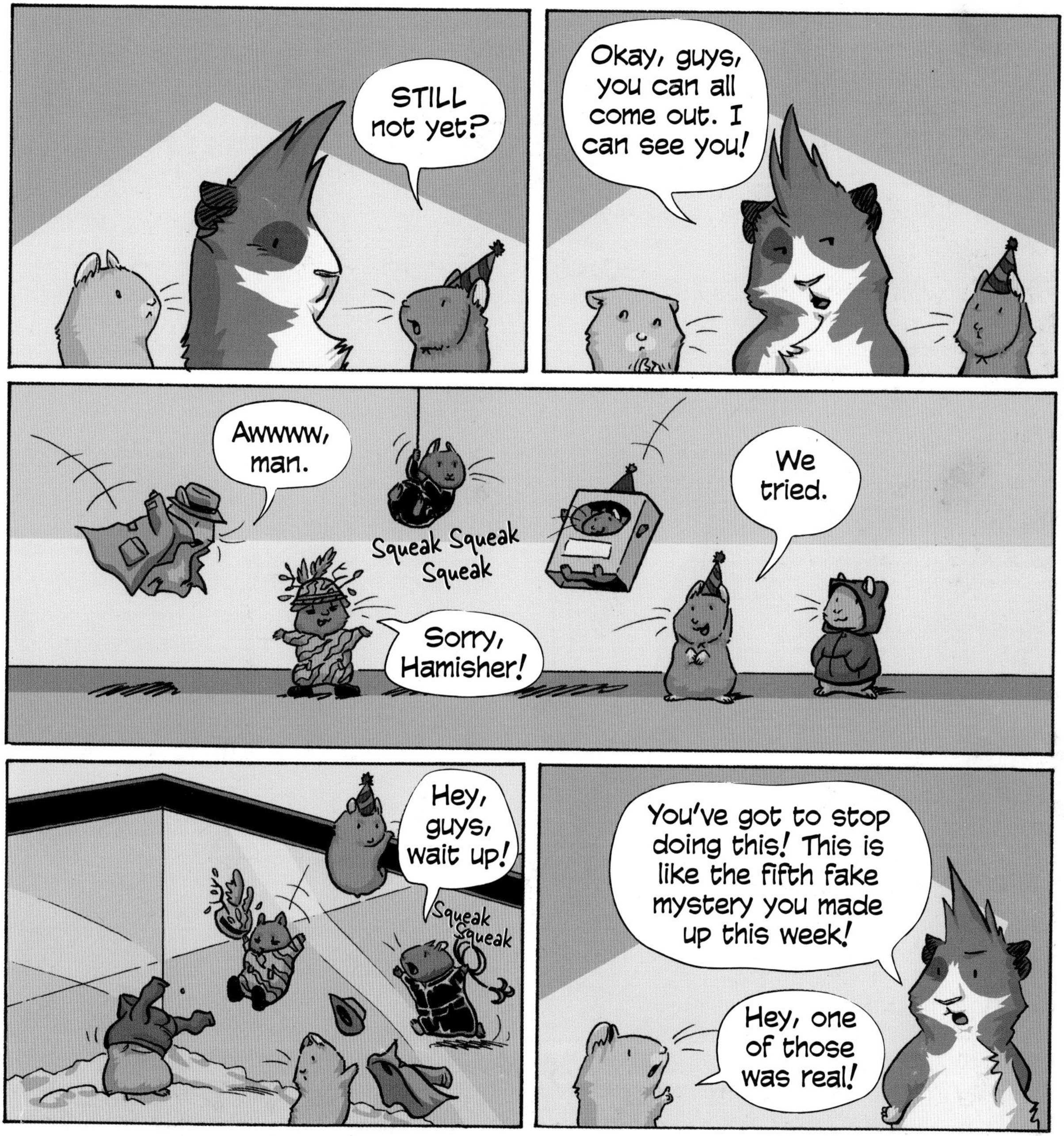
STILL not yet?
Okay, guys, you can all come out. I can see you!
Awwww, man.
Squeak Squeak Squeak
We tried.
Sorry, Hamisher!
Hey, guys, wait up!
Squeak Squeak
You've got to stop doing this! This is like the fifth fake mystery you made up this week!
Hey, one of those was real!

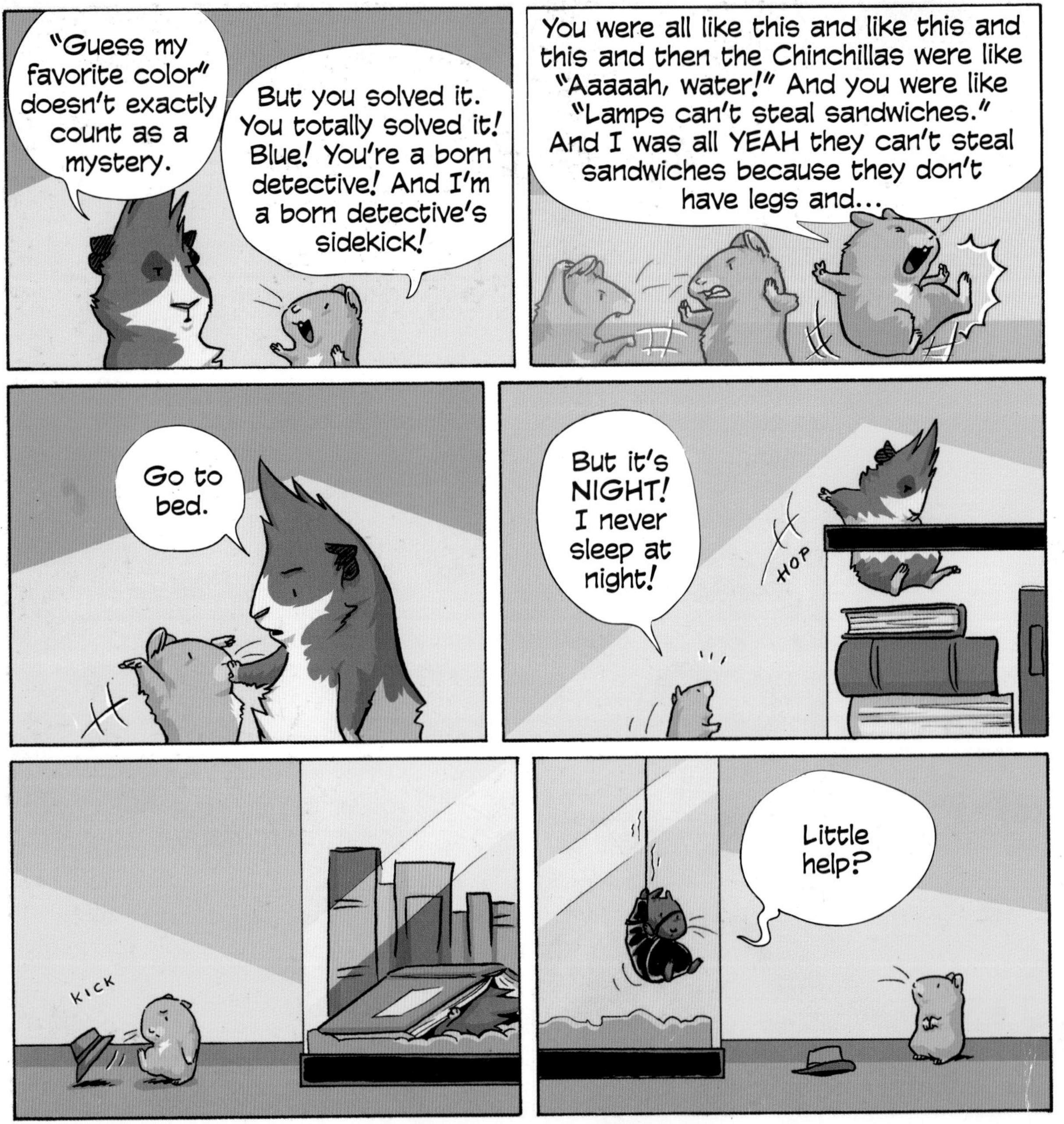
"Guess my favorite color" doesn't exactly count as a mystery.
But you solved it. You totally solved it! Blue! You're a born detective! And I'm a born detective's sidekick!
You were all like this and like this and this and then the Chinchillas were like "Aaaaah, water!" And you were like "Lamps can't steal sandwiches." And I was all YEAH they can't steal sandwiches because they don't have legs and...
Go to bed.
But it's NIGHT! I never sleep at night!
HOP
KICK
Little help?

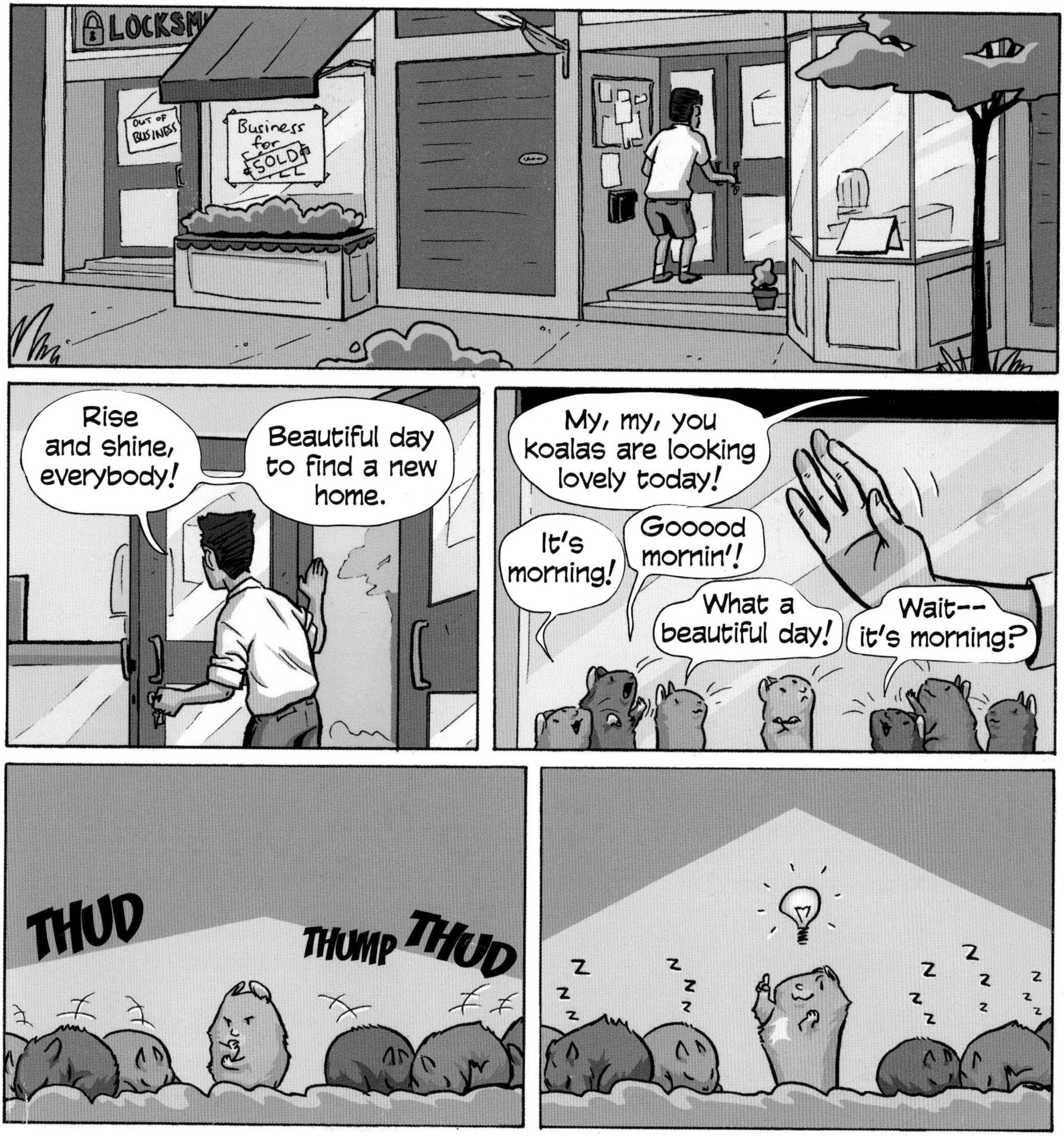
OUT OF BUSINESS
Business for SOLD
Rise and shine, everybody!
Beautiful day to find a new home.
My, my, you koalas are looking lovely today!
It's morning!
Gooood mornin'!
What a beautiful day!
Wait-- it's morning?
THUD
THUMP
THUD

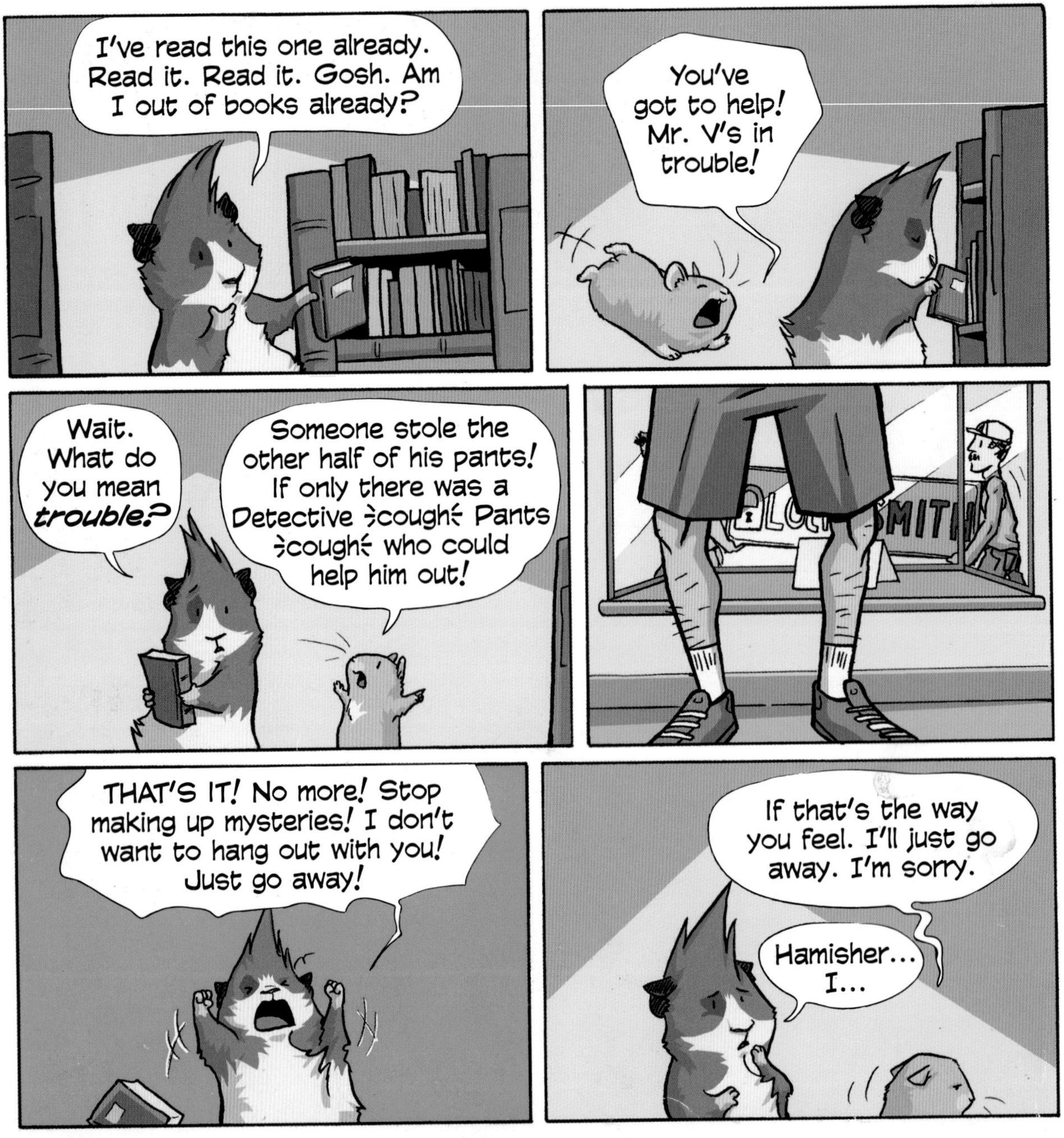
I've read this one already. Read it. Read it. Gosh. Am I out of books already?
You've got to help! Mr. V's in trouble!
Wait. What do you mean *trouble?*
Someone stole the other half of his pants! If only there was a Detective ⩥cough⩤ Pants ⩥cough⩤ who could help him out!
THAT'S IT! No more! Stop making up mysteries! I don't want to hang out with you! Just go away!
If that's the way you feel. I'll just go away. I'm sorry.
Hamisher... I...

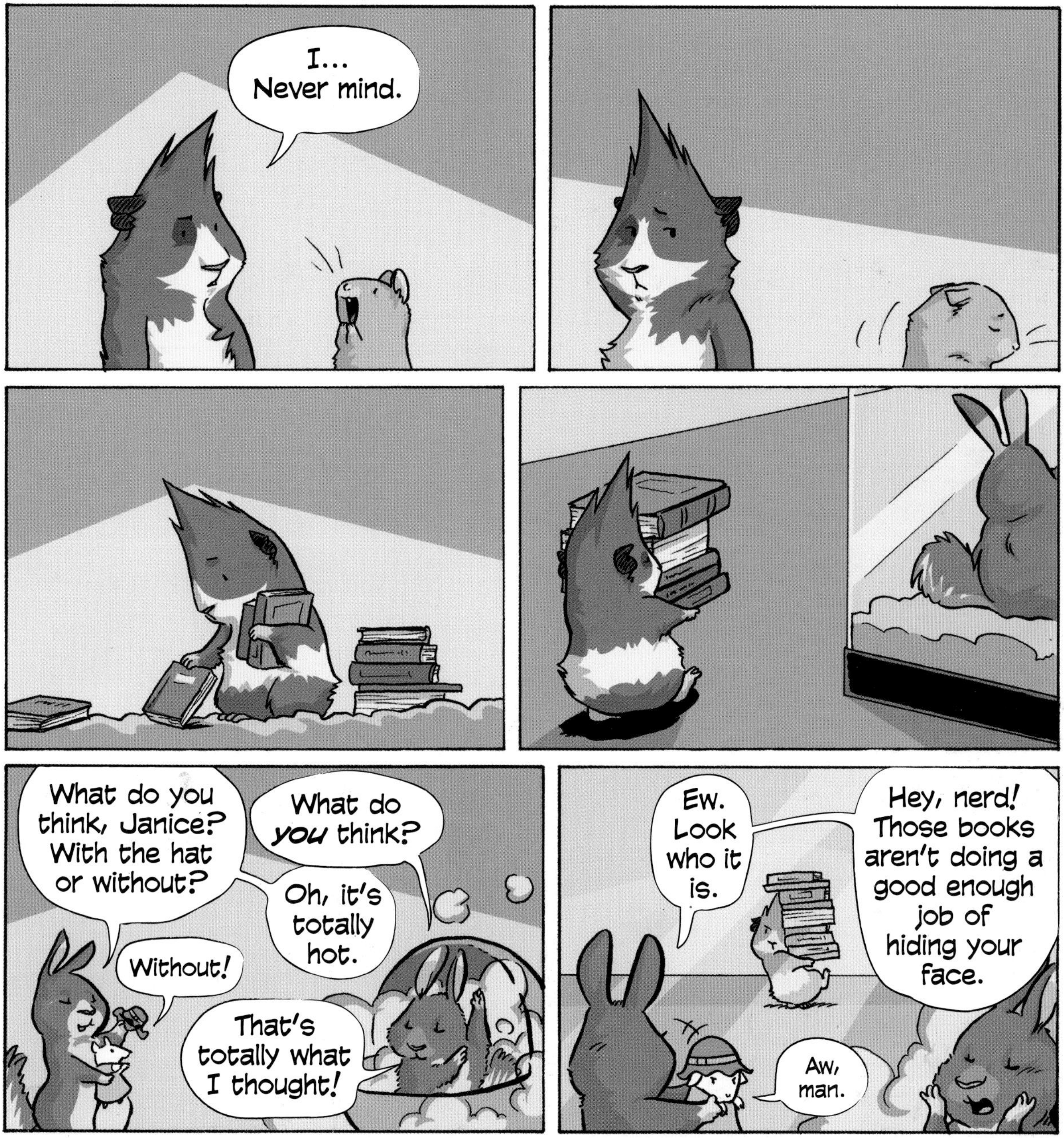
I...
Never mind.
What do you think, Janice? With the hat or without?
What do *you* think?
Oh, it's totally hot.
Without!
That's totally what I thought!
Ew. Look who it is.
Hey, nerd! Those books aren't doing a good enough job of hiding your face.
Aw, man.

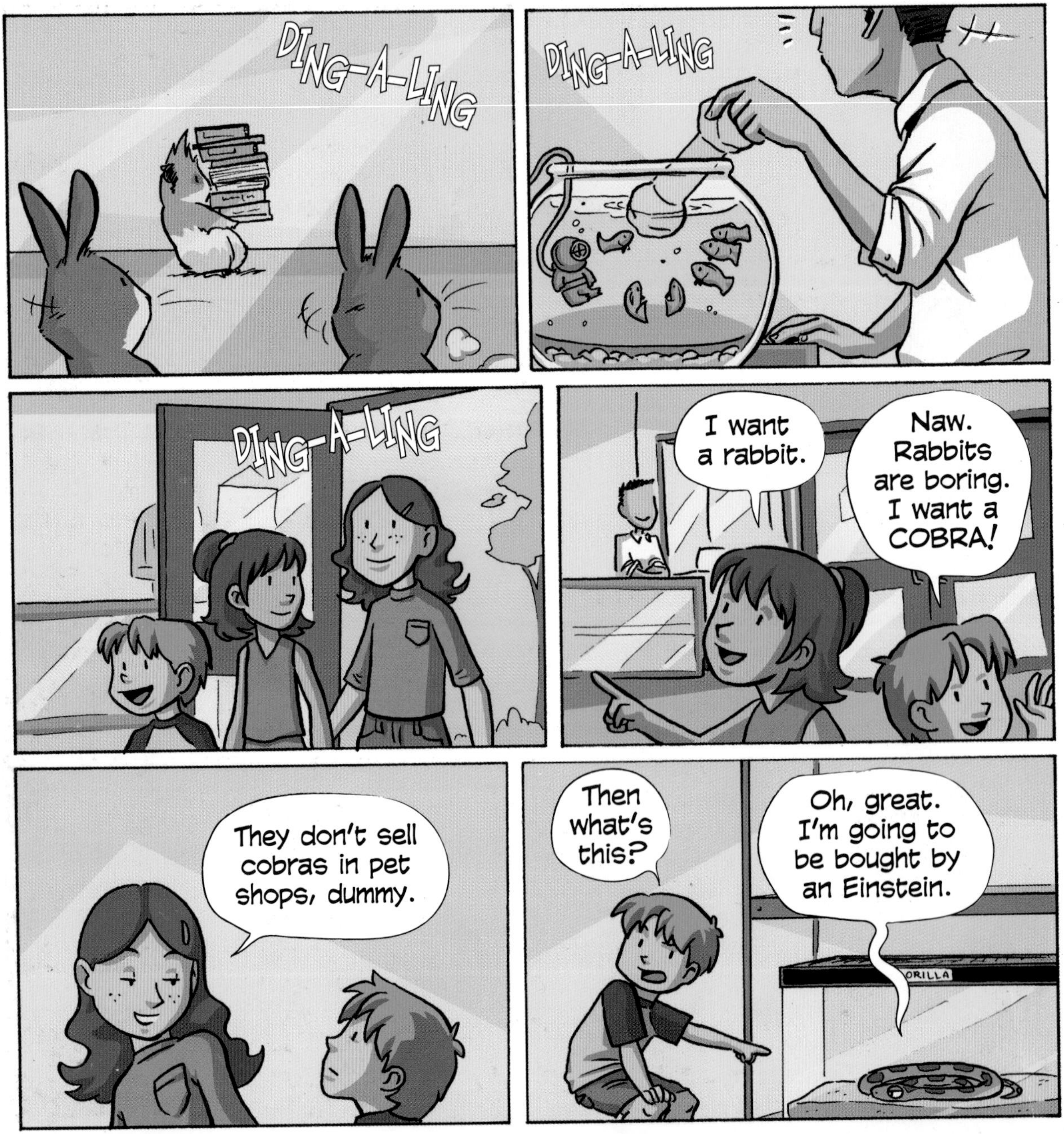
DING-A-LING
DING-A-LING
DING-A-LING
I want a rabbit.
Naw. Rabbits are boring. I want a COBRA!
They don't sell cobras in pet shops, dummy.
Then what's this?
Oh, great. I'm going to be bought by an Einstein.

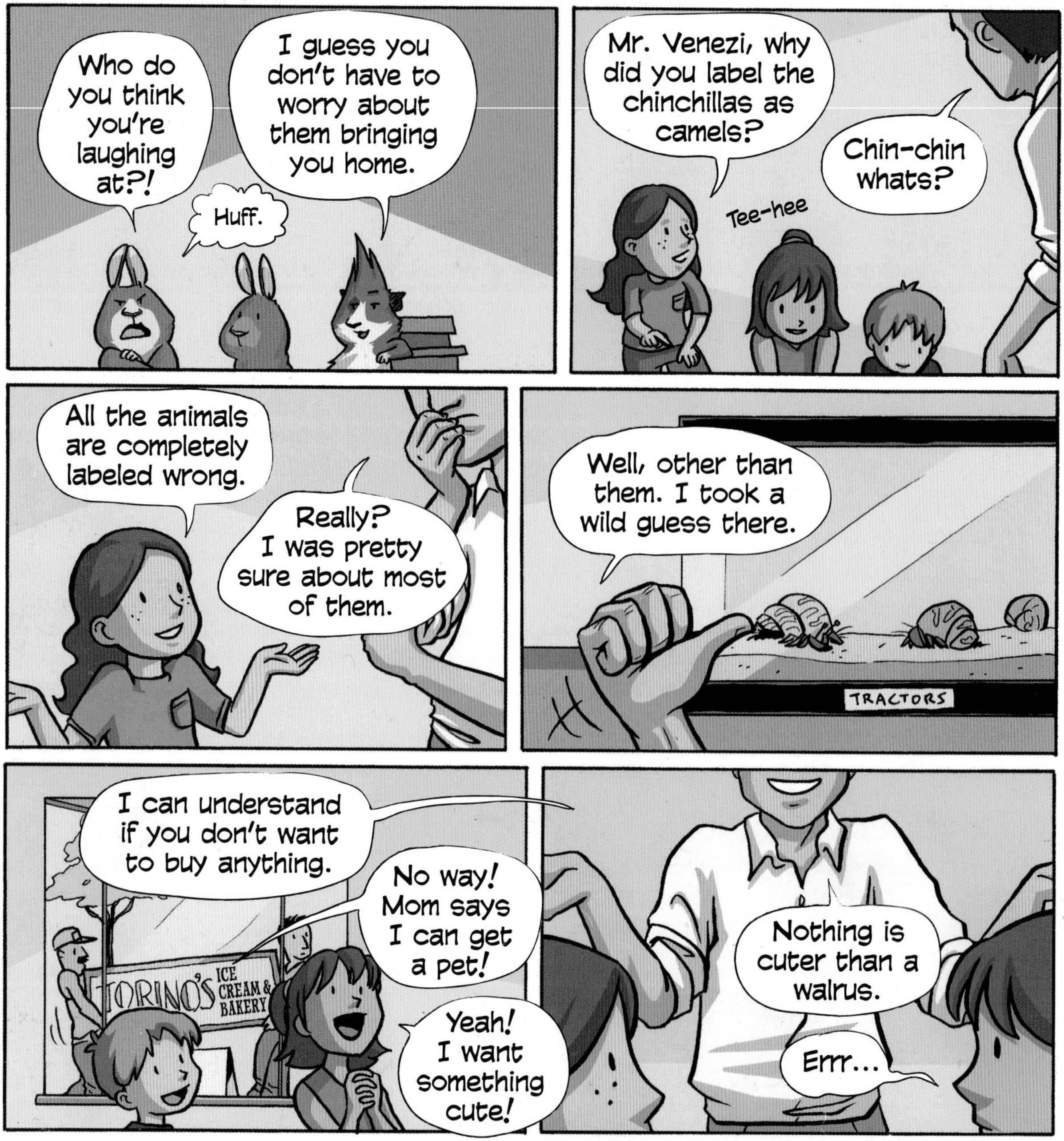
Who do you think you're laughing at?!
Huff.
I guess you don't have to worry about them bringing you home.
Mr. Venezi, why did you label the chinchillas as camels?
Tee-hee
Chin-chin whats?
All the animals are completely labeled wrong.
Really? I was pretty sure about most of them.
Well, other than them. I took a wild guess there.
TRACTORS
I can understand if you don't want to buy anything.
TORINO'S ICE CREAM & BAKERY
No way! Mom says I can get a pet!
Yeah! I want something cute!
Nothing is cuter than a walrus.
Errr...

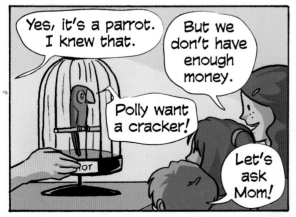

15

ALLIGATORS?
ALLIGATORS?
ALLIGATORS
And Then There Were None
Hey, Ham. Listen. About before...
No, I understand.
But I bet if there was a REAL mystery, you wouldn't be able to help yourself.
Happy Bir... zzz.
The only mysteries around here are being solved by Sherlock Holmes, Miss Marple, and Nancy Drew.
Have I met them? What cage are they in?
And Then There Were None
ALLIGATORS

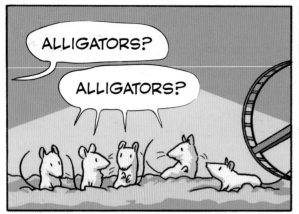

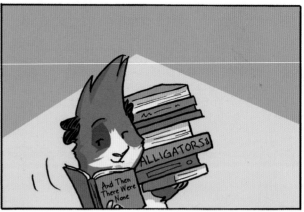

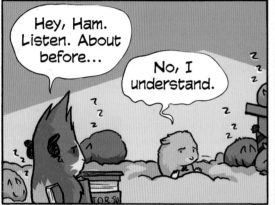

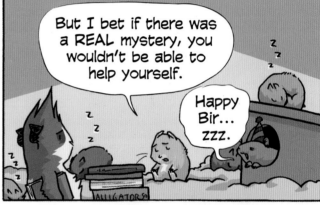

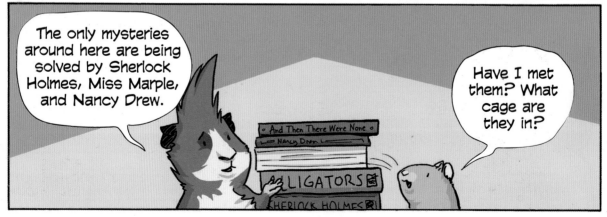

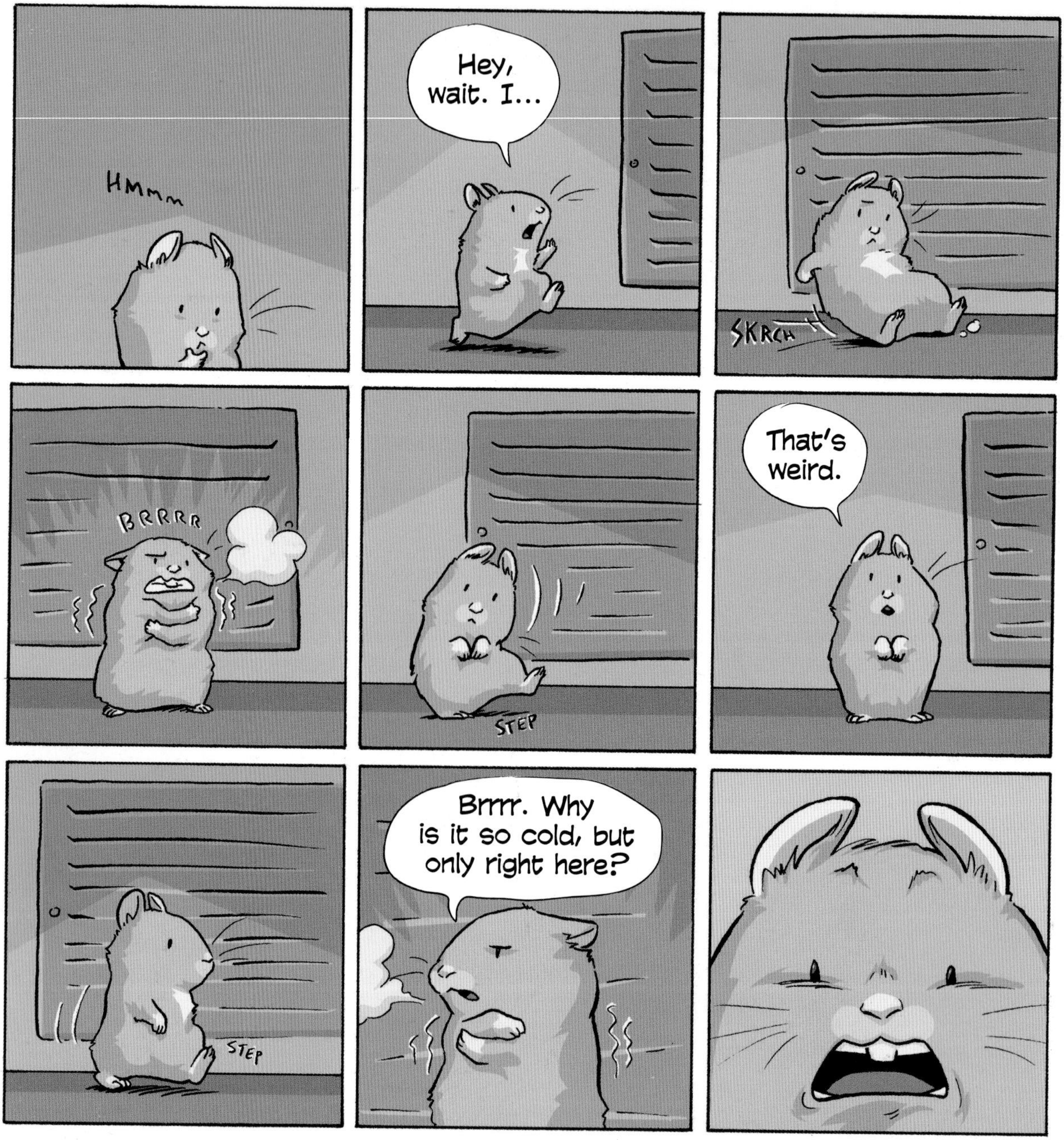
HMmm
Hey, wait. I...
SKRCH
BRRRRR
STEP
That's weird.
STEP
Brrrr. Why is it so cold, but only right here?

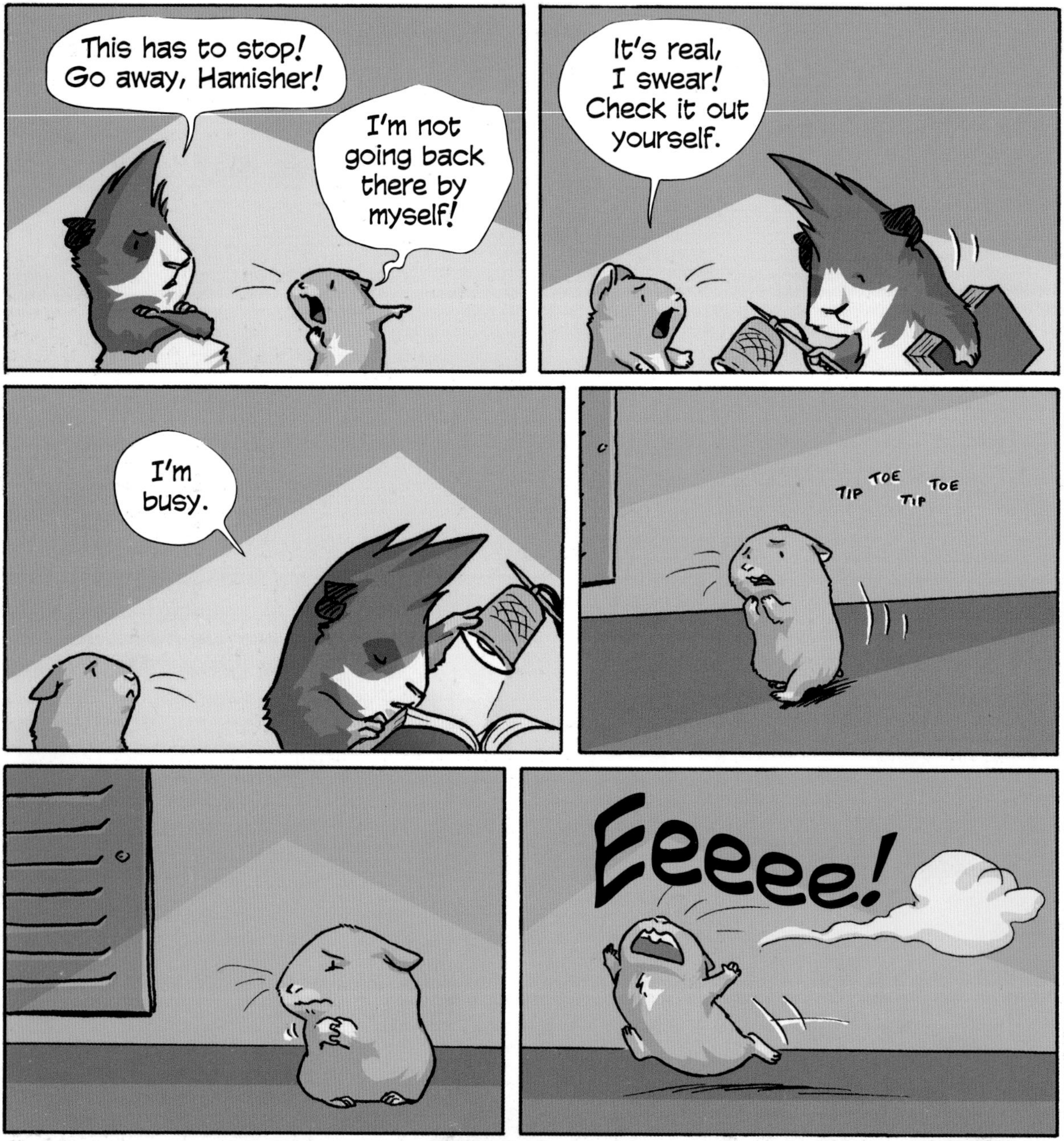
This has to stop! Go away, Hamisher!
I'm not going back there by myself!
It's real, I swear! Check it out yourself.
I'm busy.
TIP TOE TIP TOE
Eeeee!

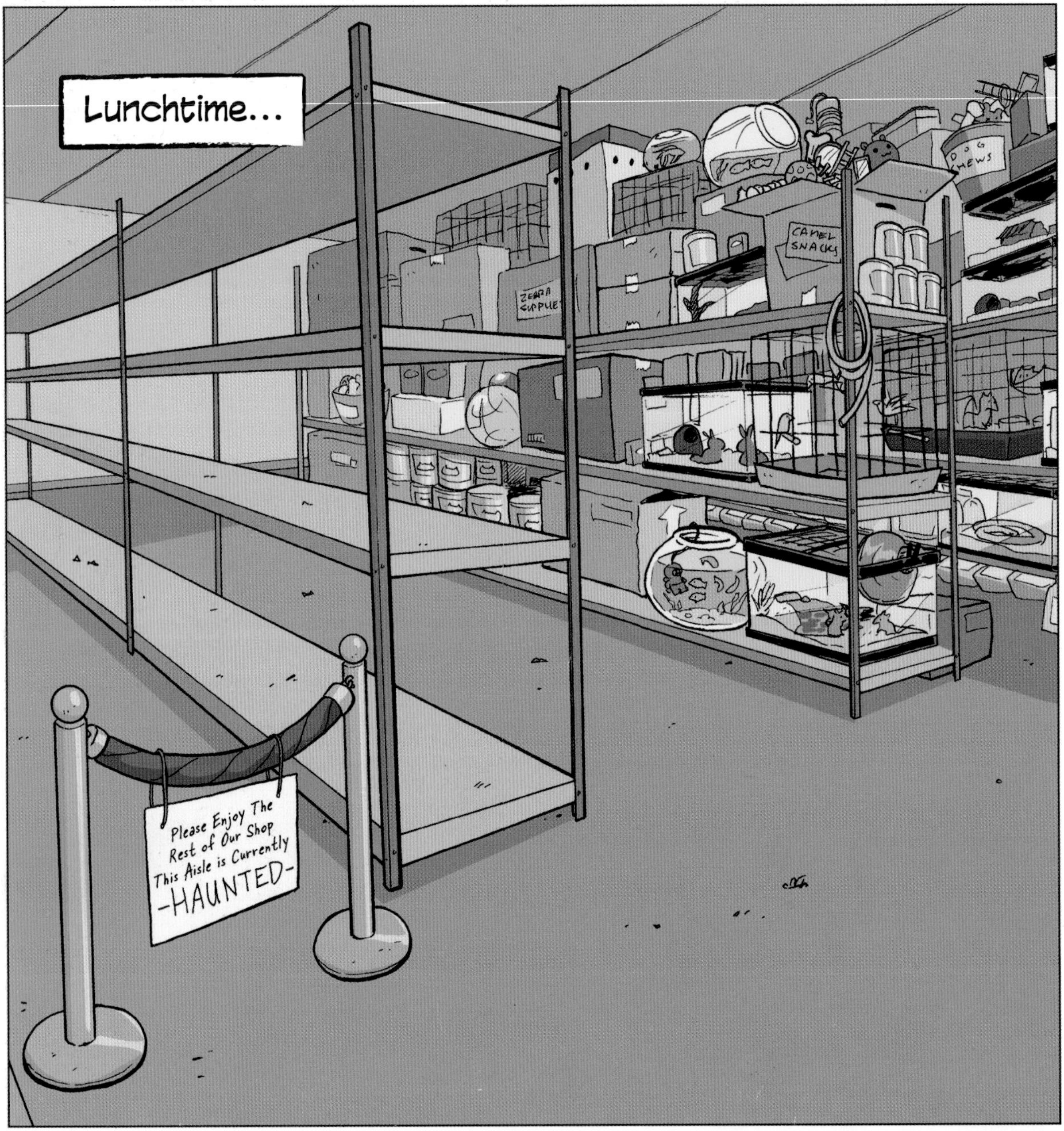
Lunchtime...
ZEBRA SUPPLIES
CAMEL SNACKS
DOG CHEWS
Please Enjoy The Rest of Our Shop This Aisle is Currently -HAUNTED-

Please Enjoy The Rest of Our Shop This Aisle is Currently — HAUNTED —

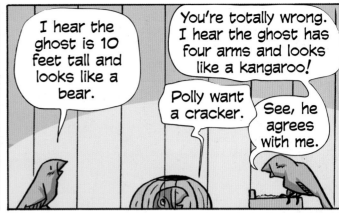

I hear the ghost is 10 feet tall and looks like a bear.

You're totally wrong. I hear the ghost has four arms and looks like a kangaroo!

Polly want a cracker.

See, he agrees with me.

I don't know why you kids are so scared. Ghosts are just things that eat you in your sleep. Nothing to worry about.

Oh. Wait...

Aaaaaah!

Clarisse...

Do you think the ghost is real?

Oh, *PLEASE.* It's probably just that dumb guinea pig. She makes things up so she can be the *HERO.*

What do you think? The sparkly pink or sparkly pinkish purple?

One of the mice disappeared last night. The mouse cage was next to the place Mr. V saw the ghost.

What?!

CHIMNEY SWEEPS

So there I was...*walking!* And then I stepped and was like "Man, the ground is cold right here." And I stepped back and was like "Man, the ground is warm right here." And then I stepped forward again and I was all *BRRRRR.* And then I stepped back and was like "It's so warm, I am going to get a tan!" It was so scary!

So scary!

So brave!

So how is Detective Pants going to catch the ghost?

She doesn't believe me.

What?!

No way!

But you got cold and then hot and then cold and then hot, and Mr. V saw it!

She thinks I'm making it up!

Are you?

Sorry, ghost! Just passing through!

Hmmm, let's see. No tails. Check! A little fuzzy. Check! Pointy hats. Check!

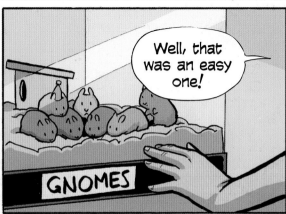

Well, that was an easy one!

GNOMES

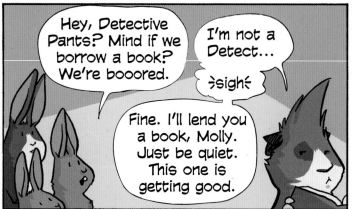

The only thing I'm here to do is prove that you're making up this whole ghost thing and ask you to stop. I can't live with those rabbits.

What?!

It's kinda obvious, Ham. You've been wanting to "solve a mystery" for weeks. It seems pretty convenient you were the one to uncover one.

I didn't do it! I swear there's a ghost!

Tell the truth.

I am! Cross my heart and eyes and legs and arms!

If you aren't going to confess, I guess I'll have to play detective one last time.

Oooh! Can I be your assistant?!

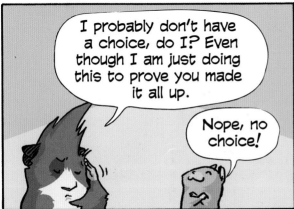

I probably don't have a choice, do I? Even though I am just doing this to prove you made it all up.

Nope, no choice!

Okay. We should start with some witnesses.

To the fish!

Well, they aren't smart enough to lie. I guess we could ask them first.

29

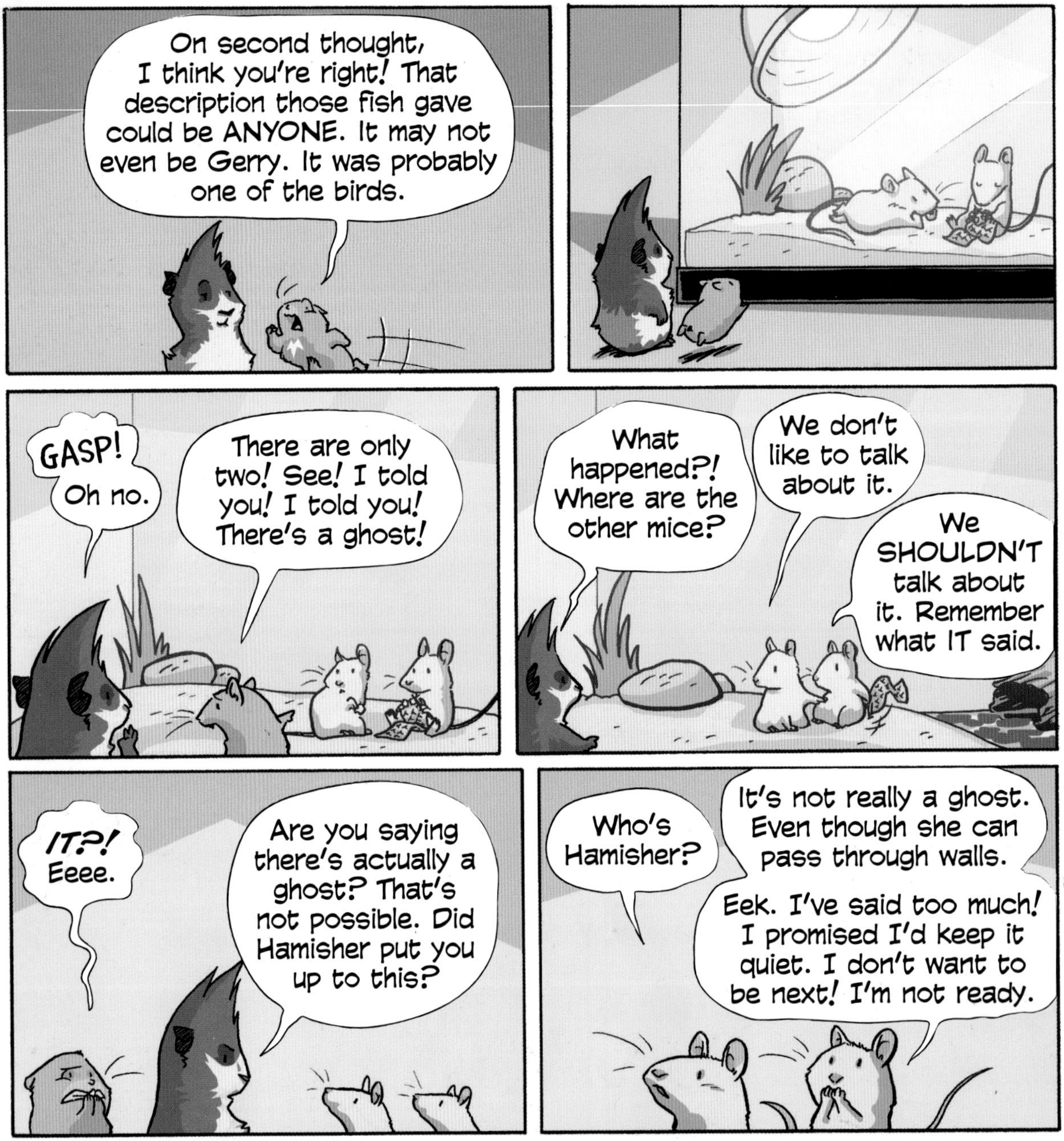
On second thought, I think you're right! That description those fish gave could be ANYONE. It may not even be Gerry. It was probably one of the birds.
GASP! Oh no.
There are only two! See! I told you! I told you! There's a ghost!
What happened?! Where are the other mice?
We don't like to talk about it.
We SHOULDN'T talk about it. Remember what IT said.
IT?! Eeee.
Are you saying there's actually a ghost? That's not possible. Did Hamisher put you up to this?
Who's Hamisher?
It's not really a ghost. Even though she can pass through walls.
Eek. I've said too much! I promised I'd keep it quiet. I don't want to be next! I'm not ready.

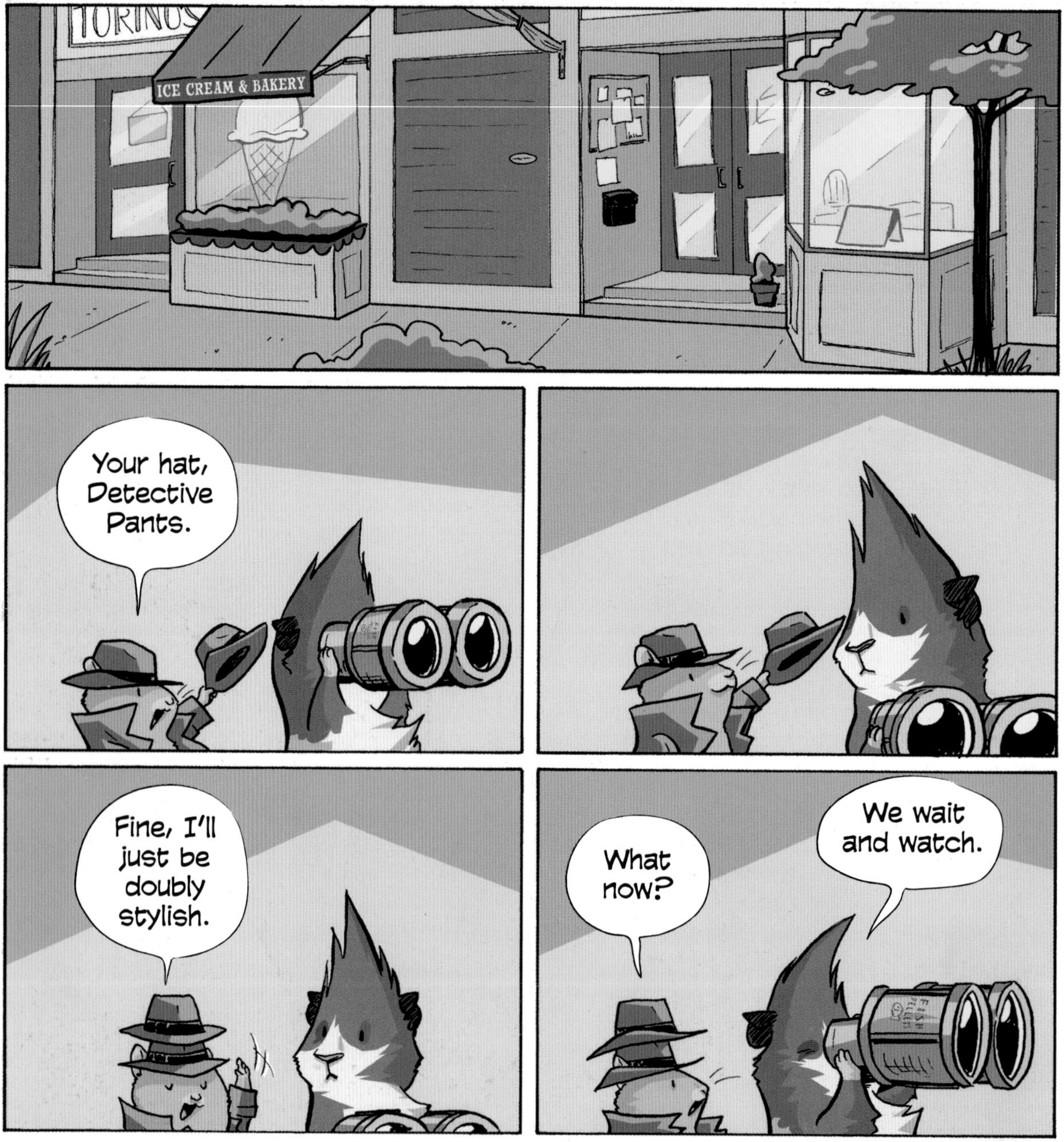
ICE CREAM & BAKERY
Your hat, Detective Pants.
Fine, I'll just be doubly stylish.
What now?
We wait and watch.

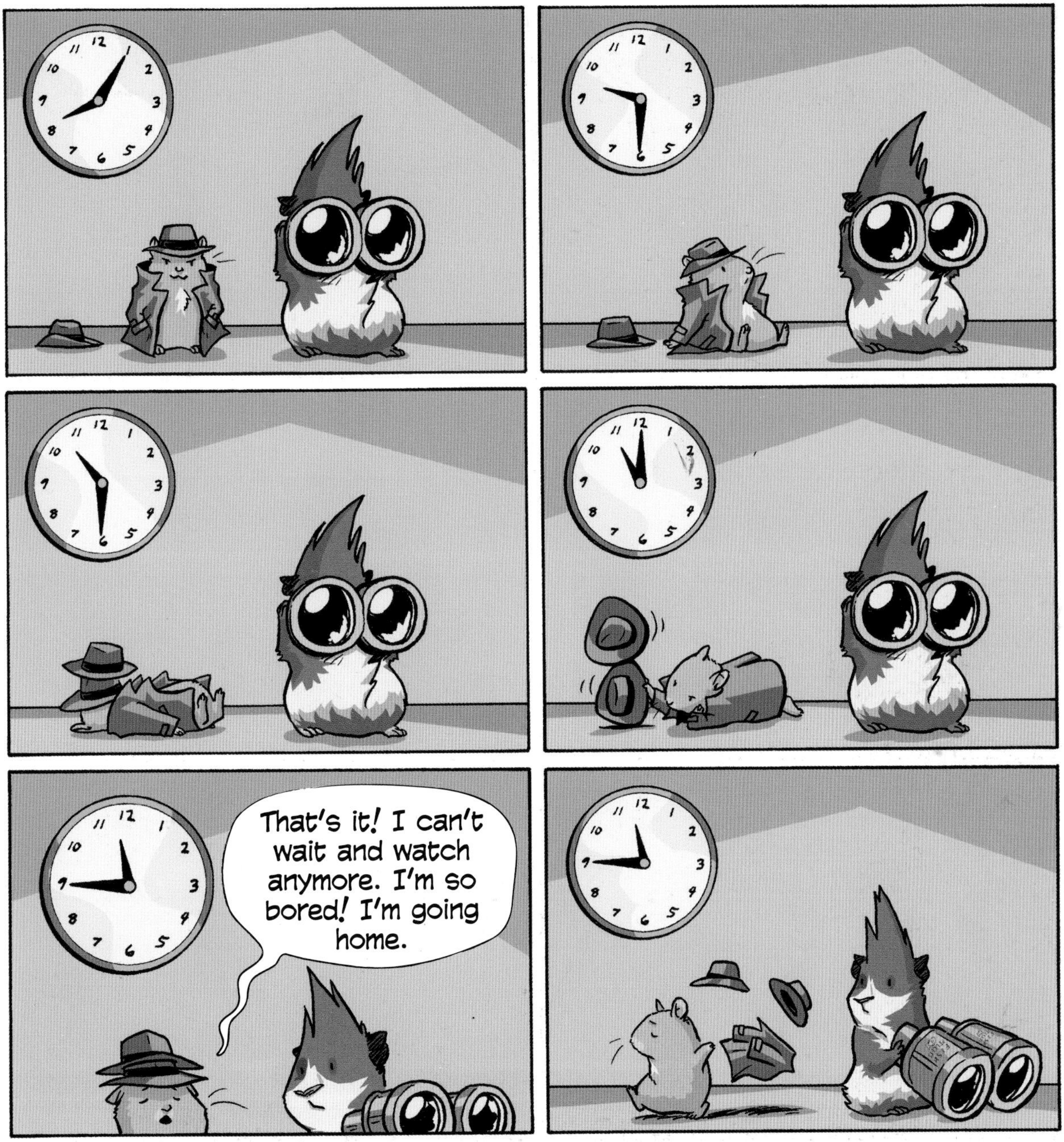
That's it! I can't wait and watch anymore. I'm so bored! I'm going home.

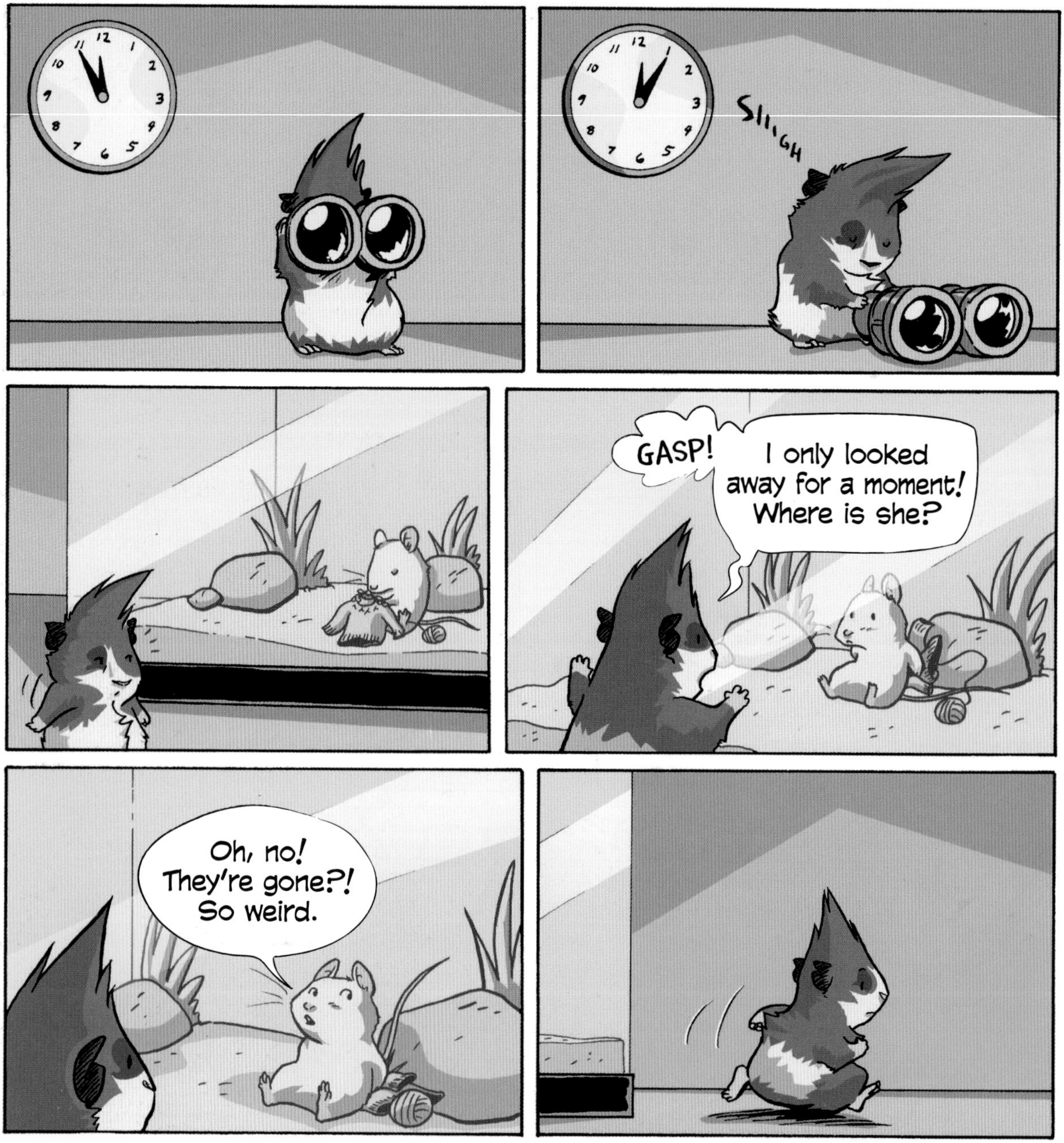
SIIIGH
GASP!
I only looked away for a moment! Where is she?
Oh, no! They're gone?! So weird.

Are those Hamisher's feet? He wouldn't...

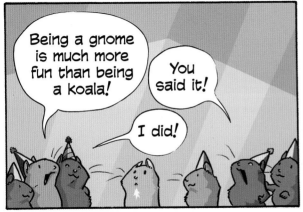

Being a gnome is much more fun than being a koala!

You said it!

I did!

What did you do with the mice?!

HAPPY BIRTH--

What?

I saw your footprints in the chinchilla bath dust, and the other mouse is gone! This isn't funny anymore.

Another one's gone?!

See.

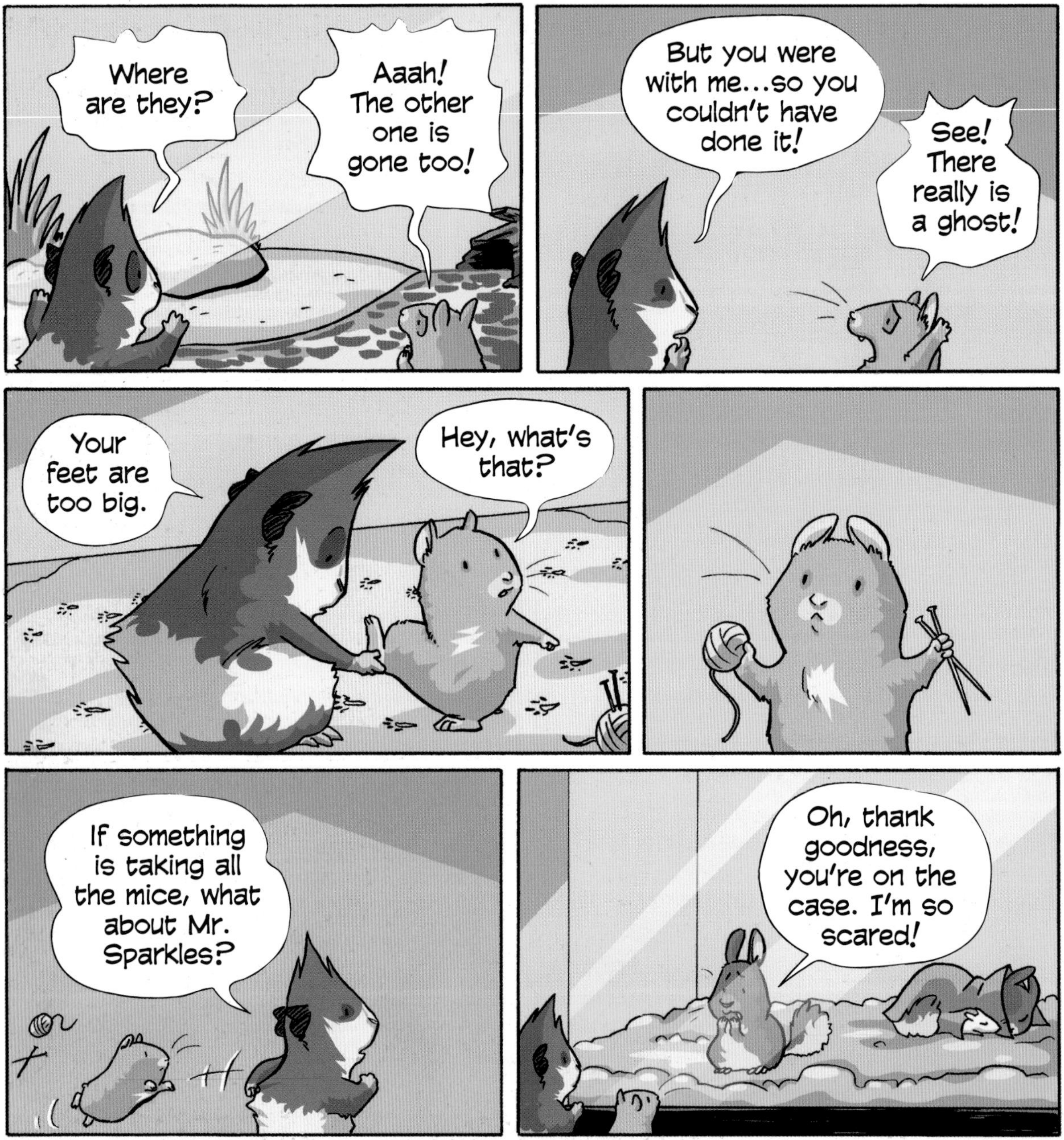
Where are they?
Aaah! The other one is gone too!
But you were with me...so you couldn't have done it!
See! There really is a ghost!
Your feet are too big.
Hey, what's that?
If something is taking all the mice, what about Mr. Sparkles?
Oh, thank goodness, you're on the case. I'm so scared!

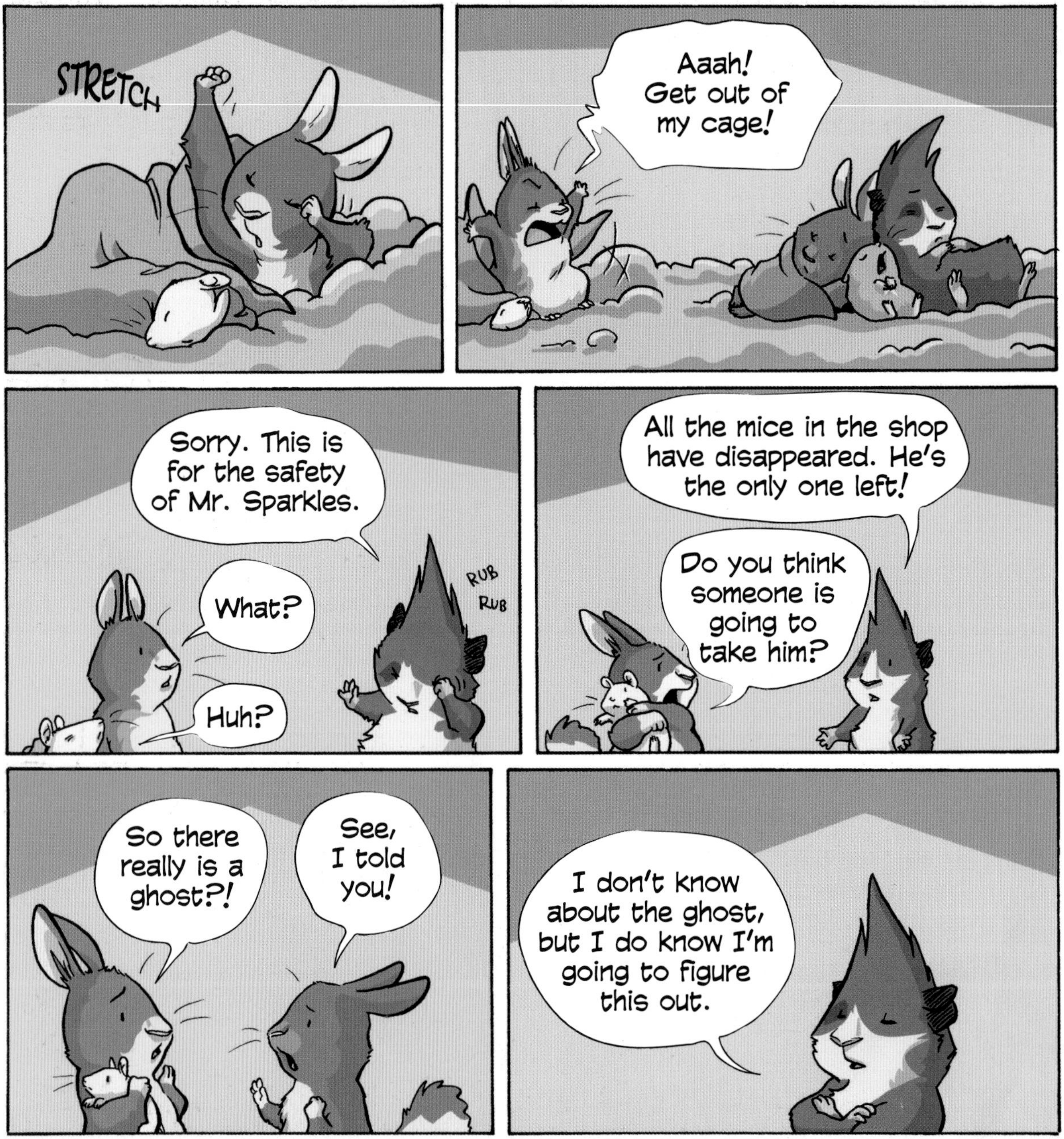
STRETCH
Aaah! Get out of my cage!
Sorry. This is for the safety of Mr. Sparkles.
RUB RUB
What?
Huh?
All the mice in the shop have disappeared. He's the only one left!
Do you think someone is going to take him?
So there really is a ghost?!
See, I told you!
I don't know about the ghost, but I do know I'm going to figure this out.

GULP

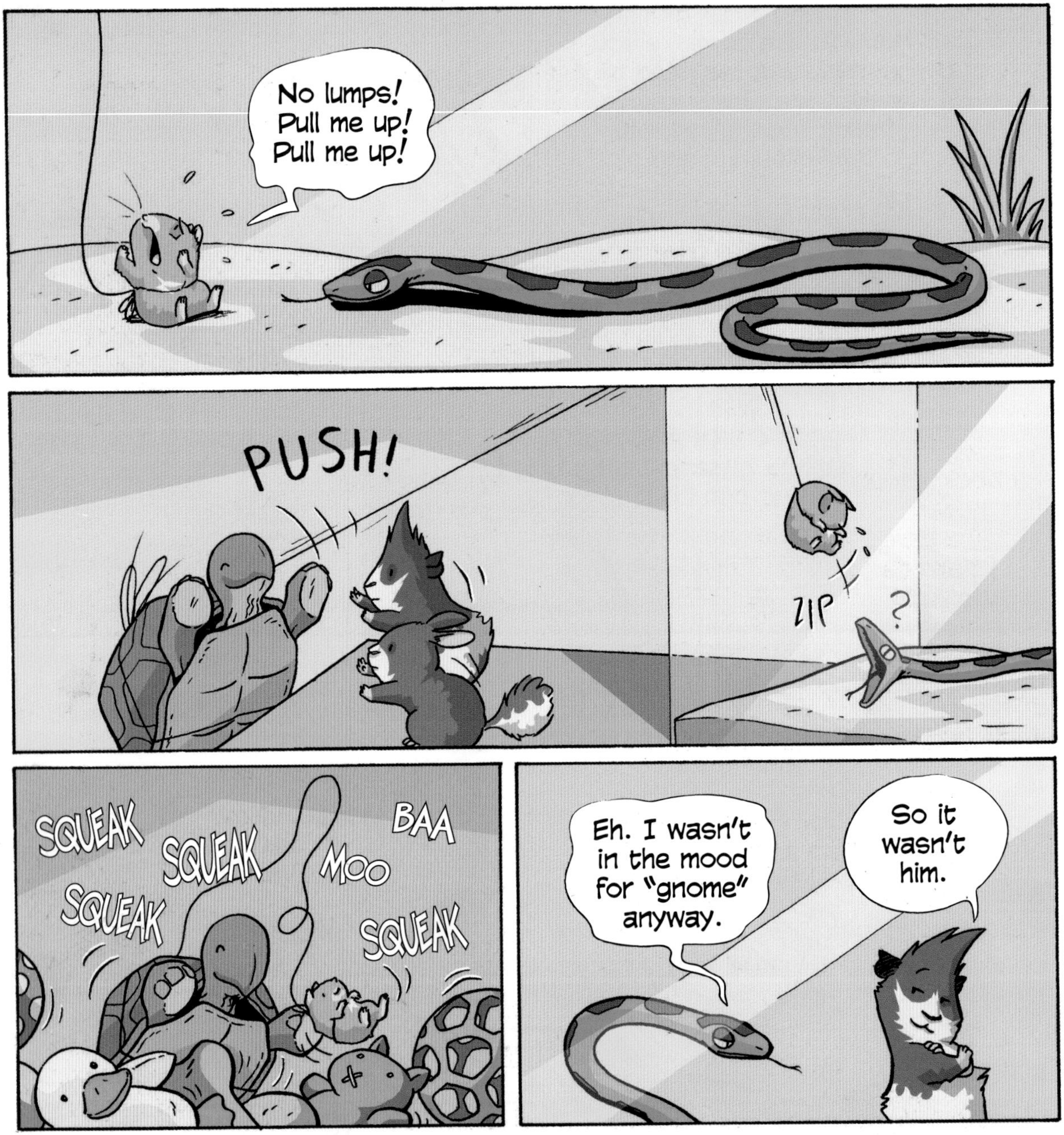
No lumps! Pull me up! Pull me up!
PUSH!
ZIP
?
SQUEAK
SQUEAK
SQUEAK
BAA
MOO
SQUEAK
Eh. I wasn't in the mood for "gnome" anyway.
So it wasn't him.

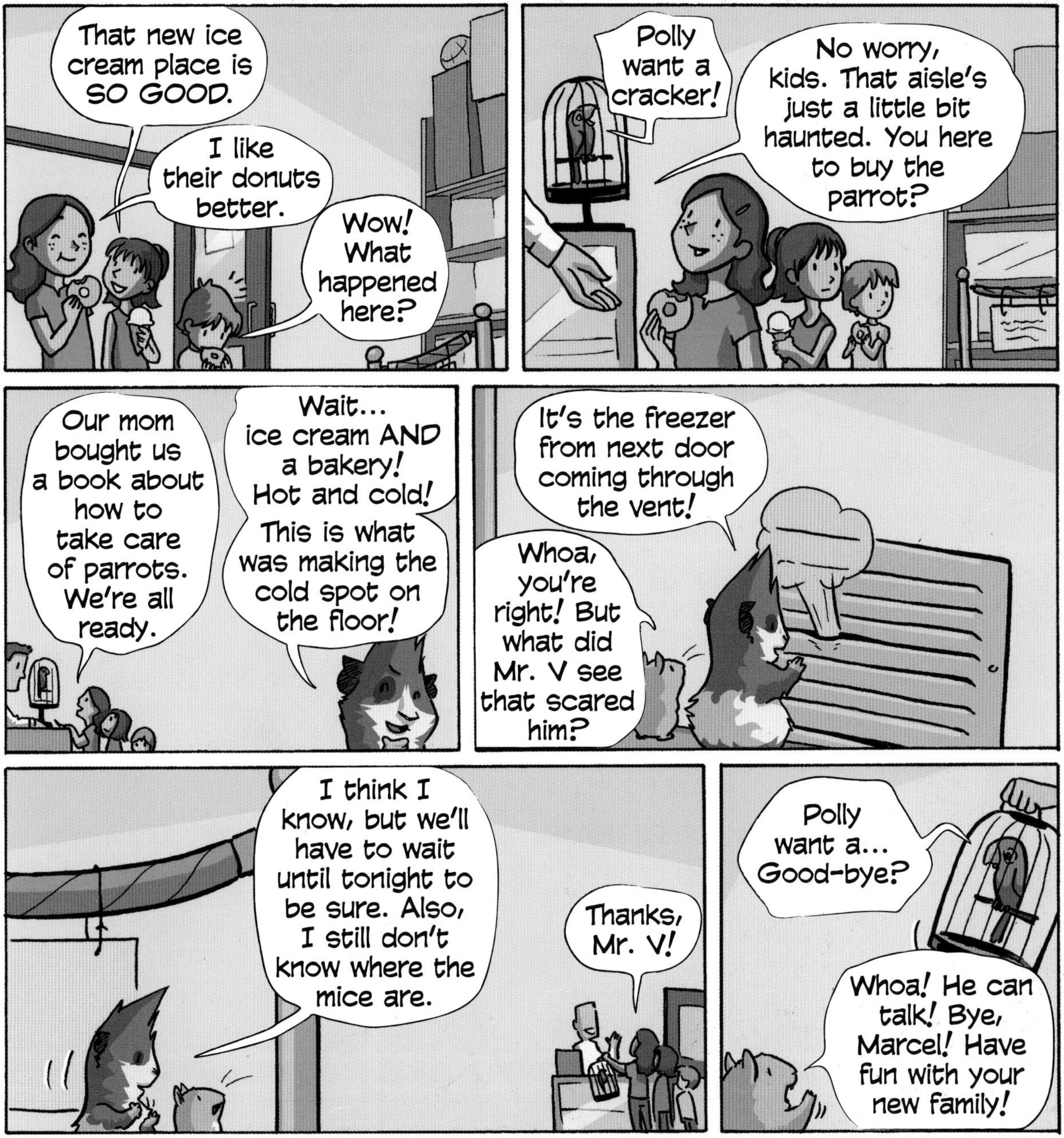
That new ice cream place is SO GOOD.
I like their donuts better.
Wow! What happened here?
Polly want a cracker!
No worry, kids. That aisle's just a little bit haunted. You here to buy the parrot?
Our mom bought us a book about how to take care of parrots. We're all ready.
Wait... ice cream AND a bakery! Hot and cold!
This is what was making the cold spot on the floor!
It's the freezer from next door coming through the vent!
Whoa, you're right! But what did Mr. V see that scared him?
I think I know, but we'll have to wait until tonight to be sure. Also, I still don't know where the mice are.
Thanks, Mr. V!
Polly want a... Good-bye?
Whoa! He can talk! Bye, Marcel! Have fun with your new family!

Good night, my little gnomes.

I know you say it's not haunted, but it still gives me the creeps!

My mistake before was that I was using a spotlight. See that light on the wall?

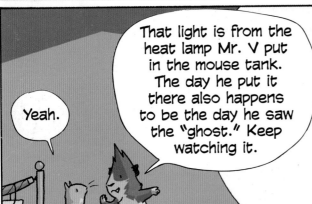
Yeah.

That light is from the heat lamp Mr. V put in the mouse tank. The day he put it there also happens to be the day he saw the "ghost." Keep watching it.

Nothing's happening.

Be patient.

Aaaaahhh!

Just what I thought! The "ghost" is the shadow of the scuba guy from the fish tank!

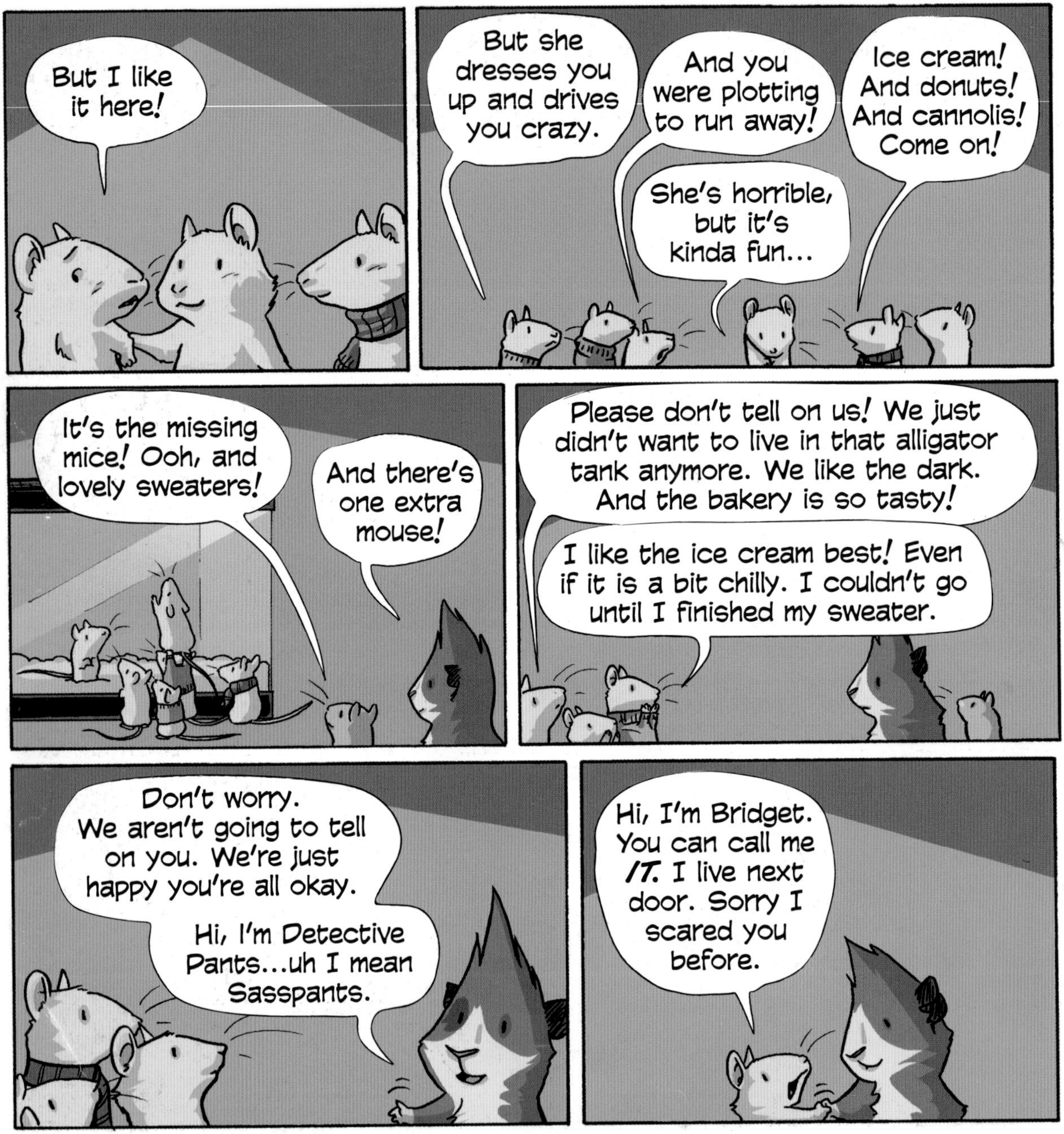
But I like it here!
But she dresses you up and drives you crazy.
And you were plotting to run away!
She's horrible, but it's kinda fun...
Ice cream! And donuts! And cannolis! Come on!
It's the missing mice! Ooh, and lovely sweaters!
And there's one extra mouse!
Please don't tell on us! We just didn't want to live in that alligator tank anymore. We like the dark. And the bakery is so tasty!
I like the ice cream best! Even if it is a bit chilly. I couldn't go until I finished my sweater.
Don't worry. We aren't going to tell on you. We're just happy you're all okay.
Hi, I'm Detective Pants...uh I mean Sasspants.
Hi, I'm Bridget. You can call me *IT*. I live next door. Sorry I scared you before.

HAMISHER EXPLAINS...

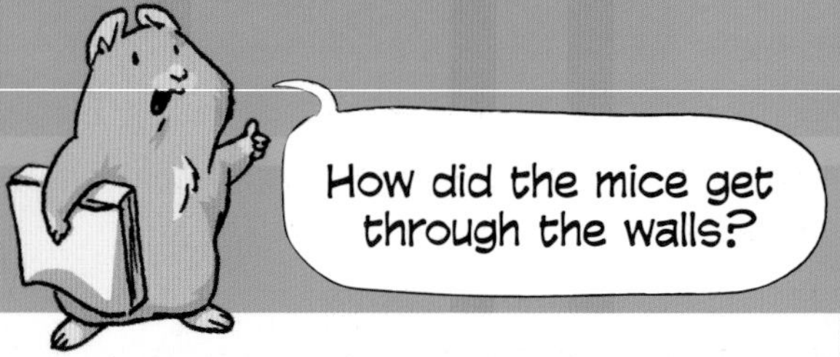

How did the mice get through the walls?

You have to promise me you won't tell them, but some days, I wish I were a mouse. Being a hamster and a gnome and former koala is awesome, and being a detective's assistant is even MORE awesome, but mice have it pretty good! And I'm not just talking about all the donuts and ice cream they're probably eating right now.

For me to fit through that tiny vent, I'd have to do a whole lot more exercise on my wheel. But mice can easily fit through! They can squeeze through a space the size of a dime. They don't even need a vent if there's any sort of crack in the wall!

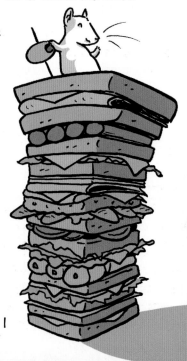

Also, if I were a mouse, I'd be a lot faster. They run 8 miles per hour. Humans average around 10 miles per hour when they run. Considering a human's leg is two million times the size of a mouse's tiny little leg, that's so crazy! Okay, maybe it's not exactly two million but we didn't have enough mice to pile up next to Mr. Venezi to find out the real number.

Mice can also climb and jump really well! Their tails may look smooth, but they actually have special scales that help with climbing. Mice can run up almost any surface—wood, bricks, really big sandwiches piled on top of sandwiches. Did I mention that mice can even walk upside down?!